Why I Love Bedtime

Illustrated by Daniel Howarth

HarperCollins *Children's Books*

I love bedtime because...

we have splashy baths.

I love bedtime because...

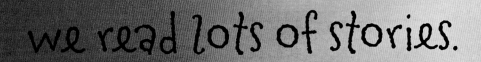

we read lots of stories.

I love bedtime because...

we sing lullabies.

I love bedtime because...

we get our beds all ready.

I love bedtime because...

I love good-night kisses.

I love bedtime because...
I love to dream.

I love bedtime because...
it's time for a good-night cuddle.

I love bedtime because...

I have a very special night-light
that helps me sleep.

I love bedtime because...

we snuggle.

I love bedtime because...

my bed is soft and warm.

Everyone loves bedtime –

especially... ME!

First published in hardback in Great Britain by HarperCollins Children's Books in 2012
This edition published in 2019

1 3 5 7 9 10 8 6 4 2

978-0-00-797701-7

HarperCollins Children's Books is a division of HarperCollins Publishers Ltd.

Text and illustrations copyright © HarperCollins Publishers Ltd 2012

A CIP catalogue record for this title is available from the British Library.

All rights reserved. No part of this publication may be reproduced, stored in a retrieval system or transmitted in any
form or by any means, electronic, mechanical, photocopying, recording or otherwise, without the prior permission
of HarperCollins Publishers Ltd, 1 London Bridge Street, London SE1 9GF.

Visit our website at www.harpercollins.co.uk

Printed in China